About the Author

The author of this book started writing late in life taking inspiration from the countryside around where she lived. Having a farming background helped in creating the general atmosphere for her stories. Her journey through life is used to create images, word pictures, situations and the fictional characters.

Dedication

Thanks to my late aunt, Jane, whose house was the inspiration.

Elizabeth Love

WHIRLWIND

Copyright © Elizabeth Love (2015)

The right of Elizabeth Love to be identified as author of this work has been asserted by her in accordance with section 77 and 78 of the Copyright, Designs and Patents Act 1988.

All rights reserved. No part of this publication may be reproduced, stored in a retrieval system, or transmitted in any form or by any means, electronic, mechanical, photocopying, recording, or otherwise, without the prior permission of the publishers.

Any person who commits any unauthorized act in relation to this publication may be liable to criminal prosecution and civil claims for damages.

A CIP catalogue record for this title is available from the British Library.

ISBN 978 1 78554 005 9 (paperback)
978 1 78554 006 6 (hardback)

www.austinmacauley.com

First Published (2015)
Austin Macauley Publishers Ltd.
25 Canada Square
Canary Wharf
London
E14 5LB

Printed and bound in Great Britain

Chapter 1

That was the beginning of it all. Eighteen-year-old Rose from Kendal was staying with her Grandma for a few days. Ormsby, in the Appleby area of Cumbria, is a remote little village where there is no bus service to speak of. A local bus company comes every Friday morning to take shoppers the five and a half miles to Appleby and to bring them back at midday.

On a Thursday night in April she had told her Grandma she intended going on the bus which meant they would be getting up at eight o'clock.

"It is a fine morning for you," Ellen said to her favourite granddaughter as they were sitting at the breakfast table. From the east facing window of the bedroom Rose had observed the clear, pale blue expanse of the morning sky as she was getting dressed – a sky that seemed to hold the promise of a fine day.

Rose went to the bedroom to get her coat and on opening the front door to the bungalow she saw that the concrete forecourt was dappled with spots of rain. The fine morning had disappeared and had been replaced by a thin mist which shrouded the landscape.

"It might only be a shower. Take my umbrella. Time's up now and you only have ten minutes."

So with "Ta ra, see you later." Rose hurried down the steps and into the drive.

The last time Rose had been to Appleby on the bus was six months ago. She was setting off to walk down to the bus shelter by the church for nine-o-clock but in fact the mini bus was not due until a quarter past nine. She was going to have a long wait there in the cold. It was a very adequate shelter, and a relic of former days when the village had been served by a regular bus. A collection point for daily newspapers where the villagers came to pick up their individual journals was how it was currently made use of. Seeing the newspapers there reminded Rose about being told to collect her Grandma's on her return to the bungalow.

It had been an idea that evolved when an elderly neighbour, living further up the road, had kindly offered to collect Ellen's daily paper from the shelter each morning and to deliver it. To circumvent the climb up the drive and up the eight stone steps to the front door of the bungalow, a purpose-made wooden box with a lid was devised to hold the paper. It had a hiding place in the corner of the perimeter wall where the paper could be collected by Ellen. It was there that Rose was to look for it.

At the shelter a young man came with a black dog. "Have you seen a bus at this time?" Rose asked him.

"No, never," he looked at his watch. "If it is supposed to come at nine, it is only just past the hour. I wish you luck," and he walked off with his paper tucked underneath his anorak.

It was still raining and Rose stood shivering under her umbrella. Another man with a bald head came by. "Have you ever seen a bus at this time?"

"A post?"

"No."

"A bus?"

As the first man had said it was, "No, never."

If these local people had not seen a bus, it must have been cancelled was Rose's deduction. Then, when it seemed fairly hopeless and she was about to give up, around the church corner appeared a beautiful white mini bus with 'Dobinson's Coaches' emboldened on its side. This was it for sure.

The driver jumped out of his seat to place a metal stool for Rose to step into the bus. Upholstered in glorious swirls of purple, mauve and blue, it was a welcoming retreat in the warmth of the interior.

"What a lovely bus this is," she remarked. "Appleby return, I want."

"That is £1.50 please."

Her hands were wet and cold and she had hold of the wet umbrella, her handbag and her gloves. She was fumbling in her purse trying to count the small change. She apologised for being slow and he saw her dilemma. He reassured her in a courteous manner but she could not avoid dropping a coin.

"I will get it."

"You sit down."

Tony was not only a bus driver but a friendly helping hand whenever needed in that country district where people of all ages and all abilities or disabilities relied on the service to do their shopping. Rose was grateful.

Even in the rain the delicate sprays of springtime greenery shone through the mist. The journey to Appleby got underway, ... past the chapel on the hill, over the little bridge and on to the lane end that goes down a gill to a waterfall and turning a corner to a long straight stretch of road. There were cowslips all along the grass verge and a bit further on, a multitude of primroses on the banks by the roadside. It was real, unspoilt country as it must have been a hundred years ago and Rose loved it.

The bus turned down a road to the next little village and picked up three more passengers. It did not have to do a three point turn for there was a convenient little circular route round and back out of the village to eventually join the main Kendal to Appleby road.

Just before reaching the market town there were three more regular passengers which constituted a full bus load. They were dropped off near the Moot Hall and Rose was advised to return at half past eleven for the bus back home.

Chapter 2

Appleby Market Hall opened at nine thirty every Friday morning and only a stone's throw from the bus stop, was a convenient shelter from the rain that morning. It was all familiar to Rose who had been several times before. There were the W.I. ladies with their carefully wrapped and carefully labelled pastries, cakes, biscuits and pots of jam which were likewise carefully displayed on a laundered white tablecloth.

It could have been the wet day or that the housewives were getting in their provisions for the weekend for it was that on entering the main hall area, Rose discovered she almost had the whole place to herself. There was a cake stall, a card stall, a fancy sock stall, a stall with all manner of household perquisites including books and small ornaments, and miscellany.

Her grandmother knew about the traders in the Market hall. There were terms according to duration as for … three months, six months and twelve months. However these terms were deviated from in certain cases. A special allowance was due to the W.I. ladies because they were outside the main hall and in the corridor. The lady with the jams and biscuits was also treated as an exception to the rule because she came every week to provide a service. It was to make cups of tea or coffee for the public. There were no facilities either but an electric point and she had to go to the staff toilet to fill her kettle. It was all makeshift but she faithfully provided mugs of tea or coffee with biscuits for a nominal charge for the country folk who could sit round a table and enjoy each other's company. That particular chill morning Rose was very glad of a warming cuppa. The R.S.P.C.A. stall, being a charity, was on a slightly reduced rate too. For anyone wanting to book a table for one Friday only the set charge was £8.00.

Rose came out of the Market Hall to discover the rain 'coming down like stair rods' as they say in the country. One of the ladies who had come on the bus was sheltering at the entrance, and on recognising her Rose cleared her throat to ask when The Courtyard Café and Gallery opened.

"You've got a cold too," Olga replied in a friendly way.

"I think it will be open but I am waiting for my friend and we are going to Taste of Eden for coffee."

Rose noticed how Olga's suedette coat was splattered with rain drops on the shoulders.

It was a colour between mustard and sage green, and there was a marked difference in the colour where the rain drops had fallen. Rose reflected that if such a good looking coat should get wetter it would never be smart again. There was a pie shop at the entrance to the Market Hall. She was standing there, uncertain and hesitating when a jovial farmer came by in his wellington boots.

"You're alright. You've got your umbrella," he remarked.

Her reply at that moment in time, quickly and spontaneously delivered as it had been, was very significant in shaping her future in after years.

It was, "My feet are getting wet though. You're alright with your wellingtons."

Rose set off walking towards the castle with the rain dripping from her umbrella. She knew approximately where the Courtyard Café was and she found the black door but it was closed. It was just a black door with no indication of any café. There was the post lady delivering letters in the pouring rain.

"Is there a place round here where you go up some steps for coffee?" Rose asked her.

"The Courtyard, it opens at ten thirty."

So Rose went back down the hill to the Post Office. She had a watch but it was in her pocket and both her mac and her hands were wet. She knew there was a clock in the Post Office. There was an accessories shop there where she bought a pair of 'magic' gloves. With her own wet gloves, wet hands and wet umbrella she retraced her steps back up the hill to the black door. It was open and through it she could see a sign painted on s strip of wood, 'Up the Stairs.' She made her way across the little courtyard and a man followed her up the stairs with a large bottle of milk.

It was as described, a gallery, and she sat down in a corner by a window that looked out onto an apple orchard in full blossom. She tried to imagine how it would have looked a picture if the sun had been shining.

"I am not quite ready to serve yet," the man said.

After a few more minutes it was, 'A mug or a cup?" Rose had already seen the poster that said, 'Mug – 80p, Cup 75p' so she ordered a mug and just enjoyed the comfort and warmth of the place until it was ready.

The walls were covered with paintings and etchings and there were cards on a display stand. Some of them were prints of local views around Appleby and she chose one of the High Cross before the entrance to the castle and paid the £1.40 for it.

"Mind the steps as you go down," the man said. She went back down to the Moot Hall and as there was still a bit of time before the bus she turned into a side street called Near Wiend. It went round a corner, into Chapel Street and into another little street called Low Wiend. By that time the rain had eased off slightly. There were two windows full of miscellaneous goods that had been donated for sale in the Oxfam shop there. She would have liked to explore the shop's interior but there was the danger of getting too absorbed and losing track of the time.

Through the half open door she could hear two ladies discussing some event they had been to the night previous. One of them was asking how her friend had enjoyed her duck. Rose didn't care for duck because they were not very particular about what they ate.

The road went past the library and she just had time to have a quick foray through the books on the display shelves before hurrying on to the bus stop. It wasn't the same driver and because he recognised her as other than a regular weekly passenger, seeing her hesitating as well, he assured her with, "Same bus, different driver."

It had rained all morning but it had not detracted from her enjoyment of the outing. The hot dinner of liver and onions on her return was very welcoming too.

Chapter 3

Burnside Road had been her mother and father's first home after they married. It was a terraced property in the old quarter of the town which was all they could afford. Rose had grown up there and had gone to school from there until she was eleven.

Then they had moved further out of town and to where the more desirable and more expensive houses lined the two sides of the same road. The semi-detached houses were built back off the road with front gardens where the first house had been straight off the street and into the living room. It was altogether more modern, residential and pleasanter but not so convenient for getting into town as the first house had been.

In her early years Rose had not been unduly worried about the lack of outlook to the front of the house for her small bedroom at the back overlooked an open space across the sprawling allotments between the two rows of terraced house. The view had been the source of curiosity that had fuelled her imagination and fantasy making. Across the dividing area she had viewed the long terraced row of back walls, monotonous grey in colour with windows all set in a haphazard and uneven pattern that came alight and diminished into obscurity every morning and every evening without any constancy.

The houses at the town end of Burnside Road were built in the late part of the nineteenth century before Kendal was very big. The town increased in size as time went by and building extended outwards along the main arteries, radiating like a spinning wheel. They differed slightly in design during the earlier period. Rose's small bedroom was a feature of that particular house, and was reached by a second stair that pivoted round a central point.

It was therefore necessary to walk on the wall side of each successive step which was difficult for a small child. The hand rail curved round with the wall and on the landing, a banister. The stair resembled such a one as might be found in an ancient tower and quite frightening looking down the stairwell from the top. It was much better for the family when they moved further up the road.

Rose counted the windows from her bedroom many times and because they were always lit up in different order she never came up with the same number. Some of the houses had outside extensions with small windows, while others had detached outbuildings making the counting a never ending game for a small child. She liked to consider where one house ended and another began for it was one long continuous battleship grey row of wall. The view of those grey walls and white window frames was so that it had the effect of making an impact on her subconscious imagination for ever after.

The flagged and enclosed back yard had been a grand place to play in her childhood days. There was a lean-to roof over the kitchen window which provided shelter from the sun or from the rain where she could read or draw.

Gladys, her black cat was never far away. The Tom feline was a fluffy kitten given to her and brought from the local pet shop in a cat basket when she turned four and it had grown up with her. Martha, her mother, had given the kitten its name in the expectation of making her daughter glad. It had turned out that way too and the incongruity of the name (the pussy being male) was unimportant. Rose was attached to the kitten from the beginning and vice versa. As a small child Rose played alone in the back yard where her kitten was almost always around. She would be heard calling its name if it strayed and Gladys mostly returned quite promptly.

If he didn't she called again and again, "Gladys" repeatedly. He always made the same return, the head poking through and then the length of the whole body squeezing under the vertical bars of the wicket at the far end of the yard. He ran to meet her when she lifted him up to hear him purr as she stroked the glossy black coat. His four paws were all white and he had a white tip to his tail. The black and white markings on his head were what were remarkable for they were completely symmetrical. The marvellous eyes were green in contrast. He had a habit of rubbing against her legs and rolling over on his back when the whiteness of the under body was displayed. He was a lovely cat and he belonged to her.

There was an elderberry bush by the white wicket which was the haunt of a particular blackbird. Rose was convinced the bird had a song especially for her. It would repeat the same plaintive echoing synchronised signature tune every time she went out into the yard. It was like a welcome, a magical and familiar sound that carried on all through the seasons. Rose was certain it was for her alone. She told her mother who agreed that it must be her daughter's blackbird. It was uncanny too.

There had been a nest in the middle of the bush but only once did they ever see the fledglings when two were hopping over the concrete flags near the kitchen door.

It was from the first house in Burnside Road that Rose and her mother attended the church at the road junction which was only a few minutes' walk. She remembered it being a friendly place but for another reason as well. It was in that church that she was given her first impressionable experience of floral art. The place was built like a huge barn with a high roof and bare walls. The entrance hall was immense and there was always a suitably large floral arrangement of dried flowers and grasses on the table by the entrance to the main body of the church.

Chapter 4

Rose had thought no more about the cheerful-looking man in wellington boots until one year later when she had a chance meeting with him again outside the butcher's shop in Appleby. It was very near to where she had first seen him. She wouldn't have recognised him but he remembered her. He had placed his order when he saw her enter the shop door, hurriedly paid for the parcel and waited for her outside.

"I say," he began, "It's a better day today isn't it?"

The "I say" bit was one quirky characteristic that Rose was later to become accustomed to but there was much more.

"It certainly is a better day," was Rose's rejoinder, and Andrew Forbes knew then that the attractive young girl had remembered him.

It was like 'faint heart never won fair lady' but his forthright manner and instinct had paid off. He had never been backward in coming forward and he hadn't known if she was single and eligible. His luck might turn for he hadn't met up with the right girl so far. He introduced himself forthwith and on discovering her name he could not help but make the obvious comment. He truly meant it as a compliment too.

"And you are a rose. Indeed you are a real English rose. The name suits you very well and I like it."

It was a promising introduction. Rose reflected about it afterwards. It was by no means the first time those words had been said about her name but they seemed to be more meaningful and honestly spoken than ever before. She smiled back at him and he thought she was as pretty as a picture. In fact the prettiest picture he had ever set eyes on.

As it happened she was staying with her grandmother for two more days which allowed her to accept the invitation and to keep the date made that morning for the following day.

During her stay at the bungalow Rose was in Ellen's care and she was going out with a young man, a stranger whom she knew nothing about. She was ready and waiting in the window seat, trying to hide her nervousness from her grandmother as the minutes ticked by on the mantel clock. It was ten minutes after the hour and then she saw the smart silver saloon car draw up outside the garden gate. This was it, her first real date.

At that time Rose who was nineteen had been left school two years and had a job working with flowers at a florists in Kendal. There had been flower arranging classes in her last year at school and she became interested and adept at the art.

She liked her work. However, she wasn't given much chance to talk about herself that afternoon for they had not been on the road very long before she was made aware of two things about Andrew. Not only did her date drive expertly and with confidence he also had a lot to say and liked to hear himself talk. By the time they were turned out on to the main Kendal to Appleby road she had learned quite a lot about him.

Rose tried to compose herself, to relax and to let herself be entertained by this extrovert young man who was, she learnt later, a few years older than herself. They were heading for Kendal on a lovely spring day, a road which was very familiar to them both. She could also almost predict what was going to happen.

She was right for when about five miles on and amongst the craggy outcrops of Orton Scar the fast talking eased off a little, the car turned off the road to a convenient level piece of ground. He was in control and she just had to put her trust in him and wait for him to order the afternoon's programme.

There are some amongst society who are natural unaffected chatterboxes and others who seem to bluff their way through life making people they meet believe they are clever, inveterate play actors. Rose had little experience of life or people but she could work it out for herself. Andrew was very much the easy going, social character. What she couldn't know so early in their liaison with her farmer friend was where it would eventually take her.

It was impossible not to be captivated by the beauty of the countryside that day. Although it was all familiar to Rose, for she had been on that same stretch of road many times, but some kind of awareness that she hadn't experienced affected her senses that afternoon. It was because of the special poignancy of the occasion and the extraordinary company she found herself enjoying. Andrew got out of the car first and she followed suit to sit on one of the stones by the car.

"It is lovely up here," he remarked.

A little further on towards Kendal there was a road leading off to the right which they could just see. Rose had never been that way. He told her about the open road over the Scar where the road overlooks the land that is covered with the craggy stones and clumps of heather. It leads onto the back road to Penrith through all the little villages.

The first village on the route is very picturesque with a famous church which is sometimes even compared to a small cathedral with its stained glass, marble plaques and a private chapel for the nobility of the district.

"I will take you there sometime to see the church of St. Lawrence."

Chapter 5

It was at that point that Rose took notice of the way her companion was dressed as well as the way he looked and the way he moved.

He had blue eyes and a fair complexion and Rose considered him to be quite handsome. They talked about the scenery and how they both liked the area. Being quite high up there was a view of the Pennine range towards Appleby where the hills were a misty blue and in the opposite direction the land dropped down into the valley. Round about them there was airiness and a feeling of wide open space where there was little signs of habitation, only the many rocky outcrops on the surface of the ground. Not much wild life either. The rocks take over and there is such a meagre covering of soil over the limestone beneath as to discourage any vegetation. The grass grows short and wiry and because there is no shelter gets the full blast of strong winds.

They sat a while and watched the white fluffy clouds floating on the horizon and hovering above them with Andrew continuing to talk. He began a long soliloquy on his passion for cars. It began with the one they were riding in, expounding on its many virtues and carried on to his knowledge of vintage cars.

"You seem to know a lot about cars."

To which he replied, "I could go on forever."

"We will go on down to the George. It opens at three-o-clock."

With that Andrew glanced at his watch and made for getting back into the car. They passed the turn-off to the right and then it was like being on top of the world. They were suddenly looking down into the valley from the top of the very steep descent, and the village far below was almost like a Lilliput one. The creamy-yellow church steeple lit up by the bright sunlight was a landmark. The sight of the village that day was like some kind of revelation for Rose, even though she had been down the same hill many times. It struck her as quite beautiful. The Inn was open and they went inside to order.

Despite the thoroughfare being a main road the village of Orton was fairly peaceful that day and generally had a country familiarity where the people all knew each other. The George had some seats at the front and in view of the passing traffic, but they found it a pleasant and convenient place to enjoy a drink that day. Other days would be busier because the Market place was where local produce from the surrounding district was brought and sold on a certain day of each week. The village had a tea room, a General Store and more unusual, a chocolate factory that manufactured all kinds of novelty goodies.

Andrew had the good sense to play the waiting game and a more secluded venue would be chosen later in their friendship. There would be other times for confidences and endearments on a future date for that was what he wanted to happen. For the immediate future he was going to find out her whereabouts and learn about her family. She came from Kendal but the distance didn't worry him too much. He would be happy to go the twenty miles to see her every weekend. He had always liked driving and felt at home in his car. As Rose was to learn later in their courtship he had first driven a tractor when he was only twelve years old. The time passed quite quickly, talking a little and watching what was going on around them. It was soon time for them to head back in the direction of home.

As Andrew drove his car back up the hill and across The Scar towards Appleby to return Rose to her grandmother's bungalow, he had a calm and decisive conviction that this girl was the one for him. She was young and inexperienced – hardly a woman of the world. He had every confidence in himself too. What he set his mind on, he would have. He knew about flowers too, and how they have to be kept at a cool temperature. He guessed hers would not be such an easy job, not like sitting at a desk in an office. He did not hesitate for one minute about arranging to meet Rose again. By the time they had arrived back at the garden gate of her grandmother's bungalow they had exchanged addresses and telephone numbers. She knew to expect Andrew at her home the following weekend.

Rose had enjoyed her outing enormously that afternoon. It was her first real promising date that had not just been a school girl/school boy affair where there was stability and security. She knew that every girl didn't get taken out in a Chrysler Avenger, and the promise that it meant was part of the incentive that led her to eagerly agree to meet again. However, she was not so untutored, naïve or inexperienced to know not to rush headlong into a commitment without thought of what she was letting herself in for. Neither was she as vain as to take the 'rose' compliment literally or other than a courteous pleasantry the day before.

When she was very young people had often made such a remark, and she had sometimes wished she had been given a different name. The name had even been the cause of her being made fun of in her school days. Her mother had called her Rosie when she was a small child. That was quite nice and her young imagination had associated the name with the rosy red apples in her grandmother's garden. Then Rose was a more fitting name in her teen years and it was her proper name. She was glad that Andrew seemed to like it. She looked forward to meeting him the following weekend with excited anticipation as any girl would who was embarking on a serious courtship with someone with some means. She began to think about the clothes she was going to wear. Her mother and perhaps her father too would see the smart car arrive outside the house and thinking ahead, she could visualise how the news of her weekend outings would be talked about.

Chapter 6

The farm in the Appleby district was three miles down the valley towards Penrith. It was fertile and low-lying but not so low as to hold water and be prone to flooding. It drained away systematically into the river Eden. Andrew's father, Tom Forbes, farmed the land in as easy a manner as was possible. It was largely stocked with cattle which were kept and fattened for slaughter. There were no sheep for he believed they were more work than they were worth. If he were like his neighbour who had two hundred Swaledale and Leicester sheep, he maintained it would be an all-the-year-round dedicated commitment.

"Use your head," he had often told his son, his only son, and Andrew had learnt from his father.

Since leaving school Andrew's life had been mapped out for him. He would take over the running of the farm when his mother and father retired in a few years time. He had never really considered doing anything else and inheriting the farm was an easy option. Some of the local people referred to him and his father as gentlemen farmers, and he supposed such a description was not inappropriate.

Some of the land was not farmed at all but was let off to someone else. It might be thought lazy but it did provide a steady income and meant that they were not dependent on the vagaries of the market or the weather. Much of the remaining land was pasture for grazing the animals. There was one large hay meadow and one that grew grass for silage and very little arable farming. It was simply productive without being labour intensive and meant that they could be self-sufficient and self-supporting without additional labour and without sophisticated machinery. In effect, they worked the farm to suit themselves.

Andrew didn't care what people said or thought. He was unaffected and unprovoked by what others were doing.

They might not be the hardest workers but if they chose not to get up early in the morning to milk a byre full of cows and to do the cleaning out afterwards, then it was how they ordered their lives. He liked to be free to go where he wanted whenever he wanted. In their own estimation they were the 'salt of the earth' as much as any of their neighbours He considered he had what could be termed 'the good life.'

Father and son might be the brains and the work force outside but Andrew's mother, Eleanor, ruled the roost from inside the house. She had always done the masterminding at Orchard Dene and Andrew had great respect for his mother. If he needed to know anything, or if his mother approved of something he was going to do, then it was a good idea. It was generally accepted and acknowledged that Mrs Forbes was clever and she was a hard worker too.

The large garden was very productive and very much a part of the farm. That was where Andrew was required to do some concentrated manual work. It paid dividends which meant he could see the results of his labour when the crops were ready so he didn't mind. He took a keen interest in it; and it was an on-going topic for discussion with both his mother and his father. They were all well initiated in the art of gardening, growing vegetables as well as flowers. Besides the extensive garden plot near the house there was a large orchard where apple trees, pear trees and plum trees yielded fruit for baking and for making jam. There was also a lean-to greenhouse for growing tomatoes, for propagating seeds and growing pot plants. It all provided an on-going occupation and interest.

Eleanor made all kinds of jam to her own special recipes and green tomato chutney as well. She made both jam and chutney for sale at the W.I. stall in Appleby Market Hall, and for show at the local Agricultural Show.

She was quite an expert on preserves for she had always done it, and the incentive of exhibiting or selling her product was what made it something other than a chore. There was another specialised craft she was skilled at and for which she had built up a reputation. It was the craft of icing cakes.

Chapter 7

Andrew had not taken any girl home to meet his mother and father until he met Rose. Because he had turned twenty four he was well aware that he ought to have a regular girl friend. He knew how his parents collaborated about this, hinting in one direction or another. They were anxious for him to make a good choice and the sooner, the better. He wanted to please them too. They were therefore pleased when their only son and heir went regularly courting almost every weekend.

Rose and Andrew had that in common that they were both the only child. Andrew was sure he had found the right girl As for Rose, in the few weeks of their courtship she had grown up a lot. They had been seeing each other every weekend, going out for dinner, to events at The Brewery Arts Centre and The Theatre by the Lake at Keswick and for little sorties into the country.

They had met in the spring when the new born lambs were gambolling in the fields and it was soon high summer. They had become much attached and for both, it seemed to be very satisfactory. Rose was inclined to shyness but level headed and thoughtful, and the two complemented each other as is often the case with successful relationships.

Andrew was never short of something to talk about for he loved words, and he loved to hear his own voice. He had, however, held back from elaborating on the one subject that interested him most which was his ambition and passion for acting. It was feigned modesty or something else perhaps but he didn't know quite how he had managed to withhold it.

Every girl or every young woman with a boyfriend who is a prospective husband will remember their introduction to his family. Rose certainly did for reason of something very unusual. It was 'The Cake.' She was always going to remember that evening because the cake was the most beautiful she had ever seen. Eleanor had a talent for icing cakes, exhibiting them and giving demonstrated talks about the subject. That was not the only discovery for Rose either.

It was set on a decorative glass cake stand on the kitchen sideboard, and when Eleanor was explaining the intricacies of cake icing Rose had caught sight of a photograph on the shelf above. Her attention was divided between taking in the art of how making the trellised pieces that adorned the 'masterpiece' were woven over the curved surface of a wooden spoon; she had her eye on a group of people that featured her boyfriend in the centre. The two ladies were alone in the kitchen, yet Rose didn't ask about the photo but ruminated on it for, with its expensive gilt frame and its central position on the sideboard, she rightly imagined it to be of importance. Could it be that Andrew had some secret occupation that he hadn't told her about? In fact it was all revealed at a later date when she discovered his involvement with the local Amateur Dramatic Society.

He was one of the most talented and important actors in the company.

The highlight of the night from his point of view was when he reappeared to take his girlfriend around the garden. It was a lovely balmy summer evening and it was very pleasant as Rose was escorted around the grounds. The vegetable plot was largely his own work and represented real manual labour and careful planning. Rose viewed the carefully maintained showpiece against the whole homestead that seemed to have an atmosphere of rural peace and harmony about it, even beauty. Andrew didn't usually get such an opportunity to show off his handiwork, and he was in his element. Rose followed him as he indicated the neat rows of peas and broad beans, opening first one of the pods and then the other for her to taste. She duly took them from his hand and tasted the half grown miniature vegetables giving an approving, 'Hmm, yes, very tasty.' The raw bean was less palatable but when the furry lined pod was opened and lifted to her, she knew she had to taste it. He laughed mockingly at her and in reply she pulled a face at him.

There were well hearted lettuces and the radishes were showing red roof tops above the ground, with alongside a small patch of grass-like cress. It all looked very healthy and the fact did not escape her that there had been a lot of digging and planting involved. She linked his arm as he directed her to the fruit bushes and the orchard.

The culmination of the evening was when they were all sitting around the kitchen table having a cup of tea with homemade shortbread and ginger biscuits. It had been an enjoyable evening, leaving Rose with a definite and far reaching impression of rural life. She could well see that Eleanor would be a hard act to follow if she were to become Andrew's wife. Not only was she on the

W.I. list of speakers and demonstrators in the district, she was the acting secretary of the Appleby branch too. In that role she had been for many years responsible for contacting and engaging speakers as well as taking down the minutes at each monthly meeting. She was very much part of the community life, a housewife and a mother.

As for their opinion of Rose, they thought she was just the perfect girl and wife for Andrew.

Chapter 8

There were three people employed in the florists, Amanda, the owner and manager, Avril who served the customers and herself. It was a team and as part of it Rose was important. Then there was the part-time lady who was on call to deliver the floral orders. She had learnt at school that you needed to have a feeling for flowers, whether you were arranging them or painting them. They were the most inspirational of all things and on many daily items such as fabric design, wall hangings and porcelain.

As a teacher of flower artistry Amanda was often called on to judge at flower shows in the district, and Rose had learnt from her. Working with them was fascinating and rewarding. Making an arrangement was like being given a blank canvas and the finished pieces were never quite the same. Flowers had varying properties, some rigid and upright, others were flexible and delicate, and their life span in water had to be taken into account. An iris would tend to last longer that a daffodil for example. Arranging them was all about shapes, colours and coordination. The arrangements varied according to their purpose, the event for the person they were intended for, and the cost to the customer which dictated the size. It was a creative art, a job that required initiative as well as common sense. An exotic flower had to be treated separately to something that was only going to last a few days.

The sources were interesting to Rose. In the spring and all throughout the summer the shop stocked flowers and plants that were in season, and many of them were grown by local market gardeners. Others came from further afield in the south of the country. The large variety of greenery species came from the local greenhouses all the year round while flowers like tulips were grown under glass as well.

Rose supposed it was the same in the 1930's and 40's as her grandmother had married in the month of February during that period, and she had carried a bouquet that was predominantly pink tulips.

The old wedding photos showed how bouquets were different. The royal blue couture dress was half hidden by the correct and accurately held position of her massive bouquet, meticulously circular in dimension with sprays and ribbons extending down the front to almost touch the hem of the long dress. Bouquets must have been considered an essential part of the attire and would have had to be made up that morning. Tulips have a capricious characteristically vexing way of altering and changing shape (both stems and flowers) which make them difficult to work with.

To a certain degree the jobs in the shop were interchangeable but Rose was mostly employed making up the arrangements on a daily basis. Sometimes however, she would be called on to help Avril out in the shop. Quite a lot of the time Rose worked on her own in the little back room, and she made up orders for celebrations of different kinds, for funerals or for people in hospital perhaps. The shop was served by a fortnightly delivery van from the south coast and that was how the more exotic blooms were obtained. The little room for making up the arrangements had a pleasant outlook onto a cobbled yard that was a busy thoroughfare as well as an outside café area in the summer. Such courtyards were to be found dotted about the town of Kendal. She could have as many as three or even four different arrangements to do in one day, and she quite enjoyed her work.

Once she had decided on and selected the flowers and greenery she would use (sometimes they would be specifically asked for) she laid them out on a long table. Then she could relax to concentrate on the job in hand.

It was in most cases likened to a blank canvas to work on, requiring a certain creative talent and always interesting. Rose was also required to deal with the flowers that came into the shop, to give a hand to serve the customers when it was busy and to occasionally answer the phone.

When they were not very busy (which didn't happen too often for long enough spells) Rose and Avril engaged in girl talk. Because they both had regular boyfriends they had quite a lot in common, and occasionally their tête-à-têtes and confidences would be interrupted. They talked about future plans, about venues, about what to wear, in fact about all things girls discussed who were mutually and earnestly courting. An untimely interruption was therefore most frustrating when the exchange had to be broken off with a hurriedly whispered, "I'll tell you later." In both cases it was extremely helpful to have a listening ear with understanding of each other.

Chapter 9

The Amateur Dramatic Society had decided on a pantomime that year but before that there was to be a concert in Appleby Market Hall. Andrew had been asked to take the all-important job of introducing the artists and generally acting as Master of Ceremonies. He had only known of this honour for a few days but he was going to 'spill the beans' when he met his fiancé.

He thought he would surprise her and was greatly looking forward to how he would impress. In fact it was not such a surprise for she had seen the photo on the sideboard the night she was at the farm. What did amaze her was how very secretive he had been about his prowess as an entertainer, knowing his exuberant and flamboyant nature. She knew how he loved talking about everything and anything and especially about himself. That was the really surprising fact when she got to know the whole story.

The concert role suited Andrew down to the ground for he could project his talent as a stand-up comic in between the artists' acts he was to introduce. He was going to be the star of the show and he had quickly collated a repertoire of anecdotes, tongue twisters, jokes and riddles intended to liven up the night. There was only a short time to rehearse any of this material for the concert was billed to go on the very next Saturday after telling Rose. He just had time to practise some of his performance on her one evening which didn't give her much chance to advise or dissuade him about any of it. The whole idea of him as a showman had been so sudden that to be called on to criticise his performance was least expected.

After rehearsing part of it he asked her for her opinion. It was really in politeness for he was as vain as a turkey cockerel, and he didn't expect any criticism. Because it was the first time he had ever been a compare at such an event, Rose was somehow aware that she ought to speak out and warn him tactfully without offending. She wished she had known earlier about this debut, his first solo performance as a presenter, as she understood it to be. She had an idea that he was inclined to rush at things like a mad bull, and that his enthusiasm and taste for stardom would overtake any caution. She had known him long enough! She did however, approve of most of the jokes which was a relief but she advised him to be a little less loud and to tone it down. She dare not say in as many words but he should be less bombastic and with a quieter manner.

It was a sort of responsibility that had been given her and she hoped she had handled it well without offending him. She wanted him to be popular as much as he did himself. She had known straight away to be evasive and not to appear over excited at what he considered to be a privilege and an honour.

The result was that he was disappointed rather than being pleased at having been corrected when he had such a high opinion of his act. He had looked forward to telling her and performing in front of her. He did, however, get the general message, and was sensitive enough to realise that his role was less important than in his vain imagination. Seeing him subdued Rose softened towards him. She put her hand in his as they sat on the sofa. She wished him luck and assured him he would be a big success. The upshot of it was that the disclosure of Andrew's great interest in acting and the theatre (as well as his interest in vintage cars) had opened up a new subject and talking point for them.

That night Andrew went home in a reflective mood. It had not turned out as he had expected. He had held back from exhibiting his ability to act, only to be rebuffed and his pride was hurt. He was miffed and a little angry. At the same time he knew his best interests were in the continued courting and keeping on equitable and romantic terms with Rose. Then he acknowledged that in fact she had been clever, wise and daring enough to speak to him of her opinion and conviction. In the end he admired her for her spunk, being also a bit surprised.

In a way it all cemented his choice and admiration of the girl who would become his wife. She was young and beautiful. He knew too, that he was over-confident, a bit overpowering and over-bearing when he got carried away. He decided he would ring her at work in the morning.

Chapter 10

There was yet a whole week before the concert and a man could do a lot in a week, so Andrew told himself. His fertile brain began working on a plan. He would invent something else to replace the mundane jokes that would act as a sketch to round off the concert.

He had picked up on what Rose had said about not liking stand-up comics but preferring duo acts. What if he were to get her to be his stooge? The little scene he had in mind would be the climax to the concert. She would be on the top of a step ladder (he knew there was such a one in the Market Hall for the purpose) as if she were looking out of an upstairs window. He would serenade her, or attempt to. He didn't have much of a singing voice but he could make a brave attempt for it wouldn't matter too much. He could see her in an appropriate dress in his mind's eye. If she didn't have one it would be easy enough to borrow one. He had in mind something like an opera singer would wear worn with short billowing sleeves and with a shimmering necklace.

He had to persuade her. It was a people's concert, given by the people, some of whom were still at school or college, and for the people. It was a small provincial town. This fact he was going to put to her, as well as it being an event that didn't happen every day. He had heard on the grape vine that all the tickets were sold too. It was an opportunity and Andrew didn't want to miss it. He would endeavour to make the most of it come what may. His act was to be a bit of conjuring in a comic way to be the finale to the night.

He wanted to say, "Ladies and Gentlemen, Rose Walton," or "My Rose Walton" preferably. The latter introduction would have pleased him but he dare not ask her permission or take the liberty without it. He had the good sense to know he would get very wrong if he did and he might even lose her. It was all in his mind and he had to put it to her in the first place. It meant a journey back to Kendal to do that, then the difficult task of making himself coherent and his intention understood.

'Faint heart never won fair lady' was never more appropriate than on the day when he set off to accomplish what was in his head and in his heart. He didn't mind the drive back over The Scar for he always enjoyed that part of the journey. All the way over the familiar terrain he thought of her and how he wanted to see her on the top of that step ladder, if only! He parked the car at the multi-storey park at the bus station and went to the flower shop. Because he had phoned earlier she was expecting him but he was a good half an hour sooner. She would be finished her work shortly so he went for a coffee over the road.

In fact the persuading that he had feared he might not do turned out to be much easier than he had anticipated.

"You want me to appear in a gown as if I were at a window?"

"Ah, yes, exactly so."

"Wasn't it marvellous how you worry about getting through to achieve your objective and then it isn't difficult at all."

He breathed a sigh of relief. She had more sense than he thought but Rose was perceptive and knew how she had upset him last time. She also guessed how much he wanted the night to be a success. Perhaps he was right and the whole idea would be better than so many 'run of the mill' jokes that were perhaps not very original. If it helped the concert then she would do it for him. Andrew could have jumped with joy. He wanted to pick her up there and then. She was a dear little thing after all and he was well pleased.

The next thing to consider was the props and he asked her approval. It was to be a massive paper rose on a massive long stem that turned into a white dove on the reverse side. There would be the words 'GOOD NIGHT' added to close the show. Rose thought how she could engineer such a placard.

But then there was something else of equal importance which was to treat his girlfriend. He would buy her the sparkling necklace. The next day he went to the jewellers. Then he had an afterthought. In the years to come, if they were together as he hoped, they would surely be remembering about the whole episode of the ladder and the rose.

Chapter 11

Andrew would not succeed to the running of the farm for another two years. Although the house was big enough to accommodate them all Rose wanted to carry on working at the Kendal florists. However, they both held the same view on marriage. Although the formal proposal had not been made, for Andrew the day could not come soon enough. It would allow him to invite his Rose for weekends, thus cancelling the weekend journeys made so often and making it easier to socialise.

With marriage on the horizon it was not only a necklace he would be looking for but a solitaire diamond engagement ring as well. He would be buying them both at the same time but only just surveying for them, seeing what was on show and the prices. He would bring his future wife to make the final choice but have them provisionally of his own preference.

Rose was staying with her grandmother the night of the concert. It was billed to start at seven-o-clock and would finish about nine. To be able to take her back and leave her with the parting gift of a boxed engagement ring would have been a dramatic and sensational end to the evening. It would be truly romantic especially if it happened to be moonlight. It was a very appealing idea but it wasn't going to happen that way. It was all going to be too much of a rush and the time was not yet ripe.

Andrew knew he had to be patient. In spite of the surprise and ecstasy of the moment the lasting result could be disappointment for her not having made it the ring of her own choosing. He knew that much about women. They were all the same about their addiction to shopping and he wanted her to be pleased with her engagement ring whatever else happened. However, what was a better idea and one that was just as much of a sensation was to make a formal proposal of marriage. He looked forward to the night of the concert with that in view.

The Moot Hall at Appleby has been there for centuries, it stands on an island in the centre of the market square where there are other relics of the past decades. The cloisters at the entrance to the church are one ancient phenomenon. There is also a bull ring fixed amongst the stone flags where bulls were tied in the days of bull baiting. The Moot Hall is a feature of the square and is a listed building. The upper floor is used for council meetings while the one below houses some small retail shops and the town's information centre. The shop owners have come and gone but the one that was there the longest was the jewellers. It sold class pieces and generally served the local community. That was where Andrew went shopping.

It was just as good as anywhere. Andrew knew that rents could be high on the high street of the bigger towns. The small, almost minute premises that hardly accommodated more than one customer at a time didn't cost a lot to rent and could compete with the bigger shops. Besides that, the knowledge of where the ring had been bought was bound to add to the intrinsic value of it. Andrew meant it to be something special and he wasn't going to stint on the price either. The lady in the shop rightly supposed that he was a man who didn't have to worry about how much the item was going to cost.

First he asked to look at some necklaces. They varied in price and were those with precious stones and those that were replicated ones. He didn't intend to pay a lot of money. It need not necessarily be a keepsake or an heirloom but to serve a purpose. It need not necessarily have great value either (it could be a memento of the night perhaps) and he chose a middle of the road one that sparkled. The lady behind the counter told him what such pieces were called which was 'A bit of bling.' That was what he wanted and he told her what he was buying it for. She could scarcely understand the odd circumstance however.

Then he asked to look at the diamond rings. He was unable to avoid the embarrassment of admitting he was soon to wed either. He had thought he might need to be out of pocket by three figures or thereabouts. However, the one that he liked, set in silver was well under that figure. He was not allowed to reserve it so it might have been sold when he returned with Rose. He paid for the necklace and explained about the ring.

Chapter 12

He had played the part of a butler and the part of a jealous husband but he had never stood alone on the platform dressed in his best suit, white shirt and bow tie. The evening went according to plan, and Rose was ready and waiting at the end to make her 'walk-on' appearance. The ladder was in place with a piece of sheeting rigged to resemble a brick wall. At the precise time she appeared at the top of the ladder dressed in a red satin gown and with the necklace just as Andrew had pictured her. He looked up and began to sing his solo rendering of "We'll gather lilacs in the spring again," with substituted words to follow.

It was a shade comical too as he hurried across the stage to collect the wooden spoon with the huge paper rose fastened to and extending from it. He took it in his right hand and threw it upwards to Rose very successfully. She pretended to smell the rose, waved gracefully to him and then to the audience with a radiant smile on her pretty face. Meanwhile Andrew engineered his white dove and the 'Goodnight' sign. He turned to face the audience with a formal bow and a hand towards his lady of the night at the 'window' on the ladder.

His jokes were well received. He went off and reappeared after every act, amongst them, a trumpet solo, a violin and a classical piano piece and some solo singers. He had a riddle about a kangaroo and a Newcastle Geordie who Can-a-giroot. Another one was a pigeon fancier who sends his prize bird to an aunt for a pet who thinks it is a dinner. It all went very well and he enjoyed himself enormously. His rehearsed trick of laughing a little at his own joke and then trailing it off was a success too.

The drive back out into the country to deliver Rose back to her grandmother's bungalow was the end of a wonderful night when he made his formal proposal of marriage at the gate. They were two happy people in love.

PART TWO

Chapter 13

It had been a wonderfully romantic whirlwind kind of courtship culminating just three weeks before Christmas They were married at Kendal in the company of their two family members and a few close friends. It was to be 'as you were,' a temporary arrangement with Rose carrying on working at the florists in Kendal.

They went down the coast to Morecambe (a little more than an hour's drive) for a short honeymoon. They stayed in one of the main hotels overlooking the sea. It was a wintry outlook in December but with each other and the rosy outlook of a life together, in effect was just as good as a tropical beach. They would inherit the farm as soon as Andrew's parents were ready to retire.

For the best part of three months Andrew had gone to rehearsals for the Christmas pantomime which was to be a Tudor themed Cinderella story. He was to play the part of court jester and after the concert experience as presenter he was well practised in amusing anecdotes. He had discussed comedy with Rose and had been directed by her in favour of slapstick. Together they had invented a duo act for the panto. In the beginning it had been his own idea, and he enthusiastically had taken a delight in describing it to Rose. It would be performed with the cooperation of a stooge and he was greatly looking forward to the event.

"It is like this you see." Andrew goes through the act for her.

"He comes onto the stage with an enormous adhesive plaster across his forehead."

Stooge. "What happened to your head?"

Andrew. "I banged it against a wall."

Stooge. "Why did you do that?"

Andrew. "Because it was lovely when I stopped."

Stooge. "Ask a silly question, you get a silly answer."

They both go off in opposite directions, appearing again with Andrew wearing a huge white bandage round his head.

Stooge. "You've been fighting with the wall again. Why did you do it this time?"

Andrew. "Because my mother wouldn't let me go out to play (or some such silly answer.)"

Stooge. "Oh, you surely don't have to ask your mother every time you want to go out."

Andrew. "Yes, I do. Are you sorry for me?"

Stooge. "I think you are just pretending."

There is some fooling about when eventually the stooge whips off the bandage. It reveals another one with the words in big red letters springing out from off the top of the head, 'KEEP OUT.' Stooge jumps back in alarm. Then the stooge continues,

"What will happen if I touch the bandage?"

Andrew. "You will drop down dead."

Stooge. "It is a drop-down-dead awful bandage?"

The stooge hops about the stage like a kangaroo. Then he comes back and accidentally bumps into Andrew, touching the bandage.

Stooge. "Oh, Oh, I've lost two fingers. Hops about holding the injured hand and eventually falls flat on the floor.

Rose approves but thinks it ought to be made even more ridiculous. She suggests that somewhere they are both divested of their trousers which are made to drop to reveal fancy boxer shorts. Of course, she was right, and he agreed with his wife. There needs to be more fooling about. When he has done some serious thinking he tells her how he has perfected the sketch.

Such slapstick comedy came easy to the uninhibited Andrew. What he couldn't do was turn a summersault but he did the next best thing. He had showed Rose how he could leapfrog over her bowed frame without scarcely touching her, something he reckoned was quite athletic for a man of his size.

Every production that went on the stage had a producer as had the pantomime. Anything performed had to be vetted by the producer so the comedy sketch had to be run through and approved.

Christmas that year was most memorable for Rose. Not only was it her first year with Andrew but it was two for the price of one.

They were together over Christmas at Burnside Road and then at the farm for the New Year. If Andrew had not been a confident, laid back character he might have been stressed out with the schedule but he managed to keep a cool head. He was a self-styled cool dude. He knew not to indulge in food and drink if he wanted to avoid getting frayed nerves. It was the Christmas that he was introduced to a girl called Claudia who was joining the company, a meeting that would lead to a dangerous liaison for him in the future.

Chapter 14

It was not until all the festivities were over did he get to reveal to Rose something about himself that he had refrained from telling. He had looked forward to the moment for some time. It was her first night at the farm when they had finished their evening meal. He told Rose he had something to show her that would be a surprise. He whipped out a head square which he had borrowed from his mother and tied it round her head. Then he took her arm and led her out across the yard with, "Prepare to be amazed." As the blindfold was removed she could only gasp in astonishment at what was there under a tarpaulin in the corner of the barn, a colossal vintage model car.

Out in the country in a farm yard when it is cold and dark, the only bit of light coming from the open kitchen door and the stable lamp that he carried in his hand made the model car look very weird. The surprise of it too, added to the surreal atmosphere, and Rose could think to say very little other than AMAZING. Eventually, as the owner lifted the paraffin lamp to highlight its specific characteristics she gained enough sense to ask,

"What is it?"

Then she was told, "It is my Essex Terraplane, as the name implies an aeroplane for the road."

Well, it didn't surprise that it had an extraordinary name.

It was an extraordinary car. Even in the dim light of the December evening Rose could see that was obvious.

"Why did you wait until dark to show me your prize?"

But he didn't answer her. It had not been in his plan to bring her there after dark. It was on impulse and somehow just happened that way.

"I will show you more in the morning," he reassured her.

Her impression of the car, so immense, so incredible with its outmoded running boards and massive bonnet that was as big and flat as the farm kitchen table top with its bulbous lamps was all she had never seen before or that she could never have imagined. It was, in one word, 'unique.' Not only did it hark back to the past, it seemed to her to represent something in the future. In fact what came to mind was 'Back to the future.' In daylight the maroon monstrosity was even more of an ultra-mega marvel.

His love of cars had been one of the first things she had come to know about Andrew. He had not told her that he frequented vintage car rallies however. He had not told her that he owned one either. Even though she didn't drive she realised that the owner of a vintage car would need to be something of a motor mechanic. She also acknowledged the fact that mechanics were clever people. It was like discovering a hidden talent, a part of him that she didn't know. It was all the more remarkable because he hadn't boasted about it earlier in their relationship. She had read about couples where one had a secret life unknown and hidden from the other. This wasn't a dark secret but something to shout about was what Rose decided at the disclosure. She began to think there could be more to learn about her husband of a few days. In fact the learning exercise would get more complex as time went by and as she would discover.

Something else happened that first Christmas together. Rose's grandmother, Ellen, then in her eighties had been a guest at the wedding but Andrew had never set foot in her bungalow. He had always waited in the car outside the gate, and to let Rose know he had arrived to collect her he had merely pipped the horn. Even before going through the gate he had admired the house and garden. The walls were finished with pebble dash, and the front door, a particularly attractive one. It was slightly recessed and set off admirably with two glass panels thus making the entrance wide enough to accommodate the tubs of flowers that were always on show.

To Andrew's eye it looked as though everything about it gelled to make a very attractive picture. It had been built in a corner of the field lately farmed by Ellen and her deceased husband. It appeared as though it had all been an integral design from the beginning. In fact a wall would have needed to have been built to complete the geometry and to create another right angle. The gate at the bottom of the drive was at an angle which added something to the general picture. There was a sloping lawn with steps up to the front door so that the bungalow had an elevated situation. When Andrew walked into the spacious lounge he was really impressed. Each of the three windows had beautiful vistas.

The window to the front looked down the garden, across the road to the field and ghyll, the second one looked over the village to the far distant misty blue

Pennine range while the one to the back viewed another field bordered by the road running down from The Scar and a beautiful old oak tree. To the front of the bungalow was the rising sun and to the back the setting sun. It was captivating.

In the curtained off dining area there were Texel sheep looking through the wire netting at the diners as they sat at the table only two to three metres distant.

The sheep resembled large woolly Teddy Bears and Andrew thought it was quite extraordinary. Ellen told how she could sit there and watch the lambs gambolling in the field. Looking out onto the idyllic countryside from within was a dream world if ever there was one.

Chapter 15

Her work was with flowers. It had all begun when Rose was at the junior school in Kendal making a wild flower buttonhole for a competition. There was a lane leading into some allotments leading off the main road just a hundred yards from their house where she had gone in search of some flowers. She had known enough to picture some dark green foliage that would act as a background to support and show up the delicate pale blue hairbells that she knew she would find there. That had been the easy bit. She was inspecting the hedgerow and combing the ground as she walked. Then she spotted a small, pretty silver leaved plant that she unearthed in its hidden away place by the gatepost at the entrance to the field. There happened to be a few red campion growing nearby and she decided they looked good against the silver. She had found all that she needed and she went home to show her mother what she had created. Her buttonhole won first prize in the junior class at the local Agricultural Show. That had been the beginning of her interest and love of flowers which would eventually lead to her successful career in flower arranging.

The next stage that followed was when her grandmother gave her a flower press one Christmas, and she had a lot of fun looking for suitable flowers. The very first ones she experimented with were the lovely hellebores (sometimes called Christmas Roses) growing right there in Ellen's front garden."

"Nip out the centre of the flower, then it won't moisten and spoil the colour," her grandmother advised her.

It was one of the first lessons she learnt about flower pressing and very good advice. The hellebores grew in a variety of colours from a soft pink to pale mauve and shades of green. What Rose found exciting was the eventual opening up by unscrewing the metal fittings at each corner of the press to discover what the flower looked like after a few weeks.

As the days lengthened and the temperature rose, the early spring flowers began to appear. They grew in the woods and lanes in the area. Rose discovered that the humble buttercup with its decorative foliage kept its glossy sheen after pressing, and the wild violet kept its delicate shape and colour well. Leaves, ferns and grasses were there in many different sizes and colours and they were interesting items for pressing in almost all seasons. Rose took her press down the lane where she had gone in search of the button-hole flowers. She knew that some flowers open their faces in the bright sunlight and that was the best time to gather them and to press them immediately. If she had carried them home before pressing, even the short distance, they would have wilted a little. The other criteria or hint was to have flowers that were not layered or of multiple petals but purely simple ones.

There was another means of pressing those flowers that were too big for the small press. They could be laid out on a piece of newspaper that had been first covered with a large piece of blotting paper. There needed to be something heavy and either a pile of books or a heavy hearth rug served the purpose as a pressing agent. She made cards with the flowers, finding that the designs need not be elaborate to be effective, and later on in her experience she learned how to use them in dried flower arrangements.

She was even able to make a broach with a tiny pressed flower arrangement which became a keepsake and a signature piece of her creative work. A pair of tweezers proved to be a very useful implement in such minute arrangements.

In her teen years she studied the technicalities of competing successfully in themed flower arrangements. There were correct ways to wire flowers and then such a device as a pipe cleaner or a cocktail stick could be improvised to strengthen or to shape a stem. There was bouquet and wreath making as well as dried flower picture arrangements. Some of the work involved the use of green coloured Gutta Percha binding or other types of florists tape. Flower heads that were small and individual could be separated from their stems and threaded onto a length of wire. A tulip stem that has a habit of curving when it is put into water might be supported by being wound loosely with a very thin length of wire.

Much later on in her life Rose was to have her personal ambition in the field of flower art. They would eventually succeed to the running of the farm and she had ideas about growing flowers there. She had noticed the garden space at the back of the house on her first visit when she had gone to meet her future mother and father-in-law. She would get Andrew to help with the digging and planting of a variety of cut flowers. She would keep pot plants in the greenhouse too. If her plans came to fruition she even had ideas of being a judge of flower arrangements at local shows. She would need to be able to drive a car but if she could learn, then she would be able to go further afield. It was all in her head and in her plans. Perhaps she might make a name for herself as the second estimable Mrs Forbes, following in the footsteps of the first but in another form of artistry.

Chapter 16

Rose knew about farm animals and especially sheep even before she ever went on a date with her 'gentleman farmer.' Ellen was well versed in the rearing of sheep for they had been the mainstay of their livelihood during her time on the farm with her late husband. Shepherding was a way of life to her and she had quite liked their sheep. It had been in the days when pet lambs, orphaned lambs as they often were or lambs that had been too many for the mother to feed were brought into the warmth of the farm kitchen to be bottle fed. Ellen was very used to such occurrences and such jobs. It had been when all the sheep on the farm were sheared by hand before the electronically powered shearing clippers were in use.

One of Ellen's earliest recollections was the day in the farm calendar when the neighbouring shepherds joined forces to shear their flock of sheep. They were brought down to the farm yard in droves with the help of the two collie dogs. She described the actual scene to Rose as a mesmerising jumble of fleeces lying on the ground alongside those that had been rolled up, the higgley piggley stools, the shearers with their upturned and sometimes frustrated or noisy animals, a general commotion it had been.

Then there was the dipping day, another dramatic and eventful day and something that the reluctant flock were subjected to. One by one they were driven into the tub full of yellow disinfectant. The frightful ordeal was the dunking overhead with the aid of a special forked implement that fitted over the neck. They followed each other to the waiting man whose job it was to immerse each sheep overhead. It was not a very pleasant job either for the one who did the dunking over the strong smelling fluid.

There was also the docking of their tails when they were young by the use of a rubber ring to stop the flow of blood. The young lambs were all treated in like manner to help them to stay healthy. If they felt any discomfort they could not protest and within a few weeks the ring was effective in resulting with the loss of the tail end. These practices might be severe but they were for the healthy maintenance of the flock. Then their feet were a constant need for care and surveillance. A sure sign of lameness was the sight of a sheep eating grass in the field on its knees. It looked odd but was like a human walking with the aid of a stick or a crutch, only the poor animal was reduced to literally walking on its knees. Attention to and the doctoring of feet was an on-going task.

Andrew knew about all those practices but he was like his father and preferred to farm the easy way. The lambing season was the most intensive and required the most skill. It meant a twenty four hour vigil to avoid the loss of any lambs as well as to protect the ewes from any distress when they were struggling to give birth. How to coax a ewe to mother a lamb that wasn't hers was a technical challenge which came only with experience and know-how. There was much to learn about lambs and eves.

The worst hazard was the snow in winter and in the Shap/Appleby district there was scarcely ever one happened without some snow storms. Sheep could survive for so long under a snow drift because the heat from their bodies and from their breath melted the snow around them. They could then live in an igloo surrounded by snow. Detecting them and digging them out always presented a problem. They had a tendency to go behind a stone wall. The snow might then drift and cover them. If the snow froze it made things a lot worse. Frost, wind and snow were a deadly combination and a farmer did not like to see his sheep suffer and die.

It was at such times as those that Andrew, like his father, could think I am well out of sheep farming even if it meant a less lucrative occupation. Theirs was the better life when they could get away with it.

Chapter 17

Their early years on the farm were very happy. Rose loved the country life with the clear air unsullied by the noise of traffic as it had been in the town. She would go out in the early morning and embrace the peace and beauty of the place, and hear only the sound of her lovely red brown Rhode pecking up the maize that she scattered at the forefront of their hen house. Tethered in the garth were the two nanny goats, one being black and white and the other a tawny colour with a dark stripe down its back. Both were equally adorable in her eyes, and she listened to their bleating voices which she liked to imagine was animal talk or animal conversation. She could watch the swallows weaving and darting in joyful celebration of the weather. She was so grateful.

Rose would breathe a sigh of satisfaction of how lucky she had been and how it had been the right thing for her. The days followed a regular pattern to a certain degree but it altered sometimes as Andrew's whim could be to suddenly decide to go off on some jaunt. He would first go out to milk the two goats which provided their daily supply. Then his father mostly came up to the farm from his retirement abode in Appleby, and they would go up the fields together to check on the cattle. They were largely Shorthorns which were an old breed, some Aberdeen Angus, a noted beef type and a few black and white Belted Galloway's. They made a lovely picture against the green grass of the pasture and the distant hills in the background.

It was quite a long walk to the far end of the farm, and they just strolled along without any pressure at all and generally enjoying each other's company. They had to check that the water troughs were full, and see that they were all in good shape. Mostly they were and it was very unusual if anything was amiss.

The cattle stayed out all summer and early autumn. They were sorted and selected in October when most of them went to be auctioned. The younger ones would be kept for another year and were housed in the large shed behind the house. When the weather turned mild enough again in the early spring they would go out again. As the autumn days came around each year and the grass had been well grazed, their feed intake was supplemented with cattle cake and silage carried to the field from the barn and silo. There was not a lot of arable farming so that there was little ploughing done in the autumn. Turnips were planted in one small field in the early spring. The grass and hay meadows were additional work in June, and some casual labour was sought. It was all a well-planned schedule which worked without much difficulty. Then there was the extensive garden to be cultivated, and for Andrew and Rose to discuss and mull over. It was a good life.

They each had their own interests, and they were happy and in love and harmony at the time. The flower craft in the florists had been hard on the hands so that it was something of a relief not to have to do that all day and every day. Rose had often had adhesive plastered fingers, and Andrew would make a mock show of kissing them better in his demonstrative way. That had been in their courting days.

Some days Andrew would take off for a whole day or for an afternoon on his own. It might be an auction or a car rally or just some excuse and pretext of looking for a piece of equipment for the farm or garden. It sometimes was to look in the hire shop for a costume for a theatrical production. He would have an enjoyable day out, coming home again to a welcoming and wholesome meal prepared by Rose. Carlisle was only about thirty miles and he could be there in an hour. That was where he went one Friday in late summer. There was a Victorian dinner at the Appleby Manor Hotel in the offing, and he was ostensibly looking for something for Rose to wear to the occasion at a place called Strutts, a hire firm in the city. Then he parked the car at the entrance to Bitts Park with the prospect of a quiet picnic and a relaxing seat in the sun. It was very pleasant with only the distant hum of traffic going along Castle Way and round towards Hardwick Circus.

The late summer flowers were very colourful with large red begonias in two beds. Another large oblong bed was planted with the smaller bedding begonias and pansies, and had two standard arrangements decked with hanging flower baskets. There were trailing petunias, ageratum and a silver leaved foliage plant with a multitude of yellow pansies again. He had bought a paper to read but there was suddenly plenty of activity around the park so he just concentrated on what was going on. He would describe it all to Rose at tea time.

Because he had a way with words, because he was knowingly guilty of liking to hear his own voice he set himself the task of making a mental note of everything that was going to happen that afternoon. He would not forget to tell her how he thought the very modern square building with its repeated rows of glass windows and flat roof completely spoiled the skyline. It was the city's Civic Centre, ugly he thought. Perhaps it was utilitarian but lacking in any architectural beauty or interest.

The first piece of entertainment was a tiny girl of about three years playing hide and seek around the Victoria monument with her mother. The lady was stylishly dressed in a white tunic worn under a long-length vivid orange cardigan. The monument, situated on a grass mound which is quite steep, gave Andrew an excellent view of the scenario. After the game with her mother finished he watched her run down the grassed mound with her dad chasing after her. The little girl then climbs back up to collect her push chair which she wheels down the slope. She pushes the vehicle back up the mound and wheels it down twice over - quite an effort for so small a child. The sight causes Andrew to reflect on family life and to wonder if he will be a father one day. The same family own a golden Labrador dog which is something else to watch as it rolls itself on the lawn, gets up and shakes itself. Other groups arrive in the park.

There is a family picnic on the grass, a mobilised chair, a stray terrier dog, another one running after a missive (ball or stick Andrew can't quite see which), a boy on a roller board and a man in a Tyrolean hat. More of interest is a young couple with a boy about twelve years on a scooter. He goes off in the opposite direction, travelling all the way round the perimeter of the grassed area of the park. Eventually he meets up with his parents at the spot near to where Andrew is seated but he cannot quite hear what is said. Each of the parents shake hands with their boy who arrived at the seat first. It had supposedly been a race as to who got there first, him on the scooter round the park and the two grown-ups walking.

Then there arrives a family of three small girls, one being a bit older than the other two. The two little ones have bikes but are too young to ride them and just travel by using their feet. The third girl is using an unusual three wheeled scooter that Andrew has never seen before and he is impressed with the adept way she motivates it, wiggling her hips from side to side in a fascinating motion. Then the last and final spectacular show is what he later describes as the Pink Princess. He has a chance to take notice for she rides her bike directly in front of where he is sitting. She wears a pink child's helmet, pink dress, and pink sandals on her pink bike with pink ribbons floating from the handlebars. She is kitted out to be a most definitely pink spectacle.

That isn't everything of interest however, for she has a little sister. She is too small to ride a bike so she has a toy animal to sit on which has to travel by being pedalled by her two feet on the ground. She bravely plays a while, being unable to compete with her elder sister, and then turns back to her mother on the seat for a cuddle. The whole scene had been a study. It had all been a free source of entertainment in the sun and very enjoyable. He could hardly explain the experience or convey the atmosphere which had been wonderful.

Chapter 18

It was not long after they took up residence at the farm, and began their individual trailblazing lives together they went on an expedition. In fact they took the vintage car to a rally at Dalemain, near Pooley Bridge, which is a noted historic country mansion. Rose was looking forward to seeing round the wonderful house at the same time. Andrew's interest was much more about showing off his prize possession and perhaps, if he was lucky, getting to know a bit more about it. All he knew was where he had seen it advertised, where he had gone to view it and how he had bargained over the price. He knew who had been its previous owner before it was bought for a collection. And he had a few handwritten details.

It had come on a vehicle transporter from a garage on the road to Newcastle, and he had been able to barter about the price because the owner had wanted it out of the way.

He planned to seek out the man who organised the rallies in the district because he knew he was an expert and an authority on vintage vans and vintage cars. The man in question owned a particular prize vehicle which he drove to all the meetings, always accompanied by his wife who was an aficionado as well as himself. If he could bump into either of them then he just might learn something about his own model. Their exhibit was a Belgian ex-army jeep and it always attracted notice. He knew how to identify it because he had read an article in a magazine about the jeep written by the owner.

Essex Terraplane suggested that there could have been a factory in Essex during the days of the early saloon car. Andrew could also suppose that his car had been something of a novelty, perhaps not built on an assembly line like the famous Model T Ford. There may not have been many of them made. He recognised that his model might even be a truly valuable piece of machinery.

"Who knows" he said to Rose who tended to be a bit less enthusiastic. She didn't share his optimistic expectation and preferred not to say an awful lot.

"It is a thing of beauty," he would argue.

"As you say, Andrew," and not show her more passive opinion of a machine that was so expensive on fuel that it could only go forty miles until the tank needed to be refilled. It was a toy to him and as they say, the thing about boys is the older they get, the more expensive their toys.

Mostly the Terraplane had been transported on a hired vehicle carrier but Dalemain was not a great distance.

They therefore planned to drive it there on the back road. A car such as the Terraplane was always going to be difficult to drive on a major road, and could not travel without being a hindrance and a nuisance to the regular traffic. They would set off very early in the morning at four-o-clock before the roads got busy. Andrew had the car out of the barn several times for a practise run before the day of the rally. He polished the body, rubbed the metal casing on the lamps until it shone and oiled the engine. He had it looking smart and turned out to perfection as a manikin might be prepared before she went on the cat walk.

They rose early and dressed in suitable clothing which, in Andrew's case was always casual wear because he never could be sure if the vintage car would not be temperamental and break down. It might need some adjustment on the road and that was always a hazard even after the extreme care taken to avoid such an accident or incident. They got the car onto the road with Rose looking like a lady of the era to which it belonged. They were travelling on the back road from Penrith when the house came into view about one and a half hours after they had left the farm. It was just at the dawning of the day and they were one of the first few vehicles to drive onto the field at the front. The extensive grounds had once been a deer park too.

Rose thought the house was magnificent in such a splendid setting. It most definitely was a grand country residence to compare with those estates as described in the chapters of Jane Austin's novels.

Later on in the day she got to go through the house and that was a treat she would not have liked to miss.

The mansion dated back to medieval times with additions and alterations by the later members of the Hassell family, first purchased by one of them in the reign of Charles II. The pale pink sandstone façade stood out as distinctive and the interior was equally impressive. The spacious entrance hall opened onto a fine staircase with an elaborately carved wooden handrail with a tassel motive and a tiled floor. There were other outstanding features such as a Chinese room, another magnificent drawing room, a panelled room with an Elizabethan fretwork ceiling, four poster beds in the bedrooms, a nursery with the family's original toys still on show, a kitchen with old utensils, a stable courtyard outside with original cobbles and many important portraits and furniture throughout.

The whole day had been a truly wonderful and exciting experience for them both when they arrived back at nine-o-clock that night. Andrew wasn't much wiser about his vintage model. He had been advised that it was probably a one off product or an experiment at the time by someone with a vision to make a showy design and commission what had been thought an elegant gentleman's machine. It could have been someone with a French connection; also someone with useful connections in the motor manufacturing business and who had plenty of money at his disposal. He parked his car in its place in the barn in readiness for another journey to the next rally.

Chapter 19

It was while they were rehearsing for a new play that Andrew's good reputation was put to the test. He had been cast as the leading man and Claudia, whom he had first met five years back, was playing his wilful and errant wife. It was a little known French drama, 'The Truth,' that had been translated into English, and there was a scene where the two characters acted out a heated husband and wife argument.

Although the producer had the different actors in the company reading the two parts in the early stage of the production, there was no doubt the obvious choice was going to be Andrew and Claudia. In fact they seemed to be made for the parts with their good looks and acting ability. Claudia even looked a bit French with her dark, handsome features and her chic, well groomed appearance. The audience would love them thought the producer.

It all went well at the beginning. However, as the weeks passed, having to work so closely with Claudia, both at rehearsal and in between when they spoke on the phone about the play was just to prove too much of a strain and a test for Andrew not to let himself be carried away and getting emotionally entangled.

There came the stage when they had both learned their parts and were word perfect but they became so disorientated with the drama and their attraction to each other, that they almost always ended up improvising. The result was that the angry scene was never performed the same way twice.

It gradually became clear to the rest of the cast that they were attracted to each other but all any of them could do was to look on and to anxiously observe. Andrew knew enough and had read enough to know that a man can fall in love with his leading lady on a film set. Here he found himself in the same sort of situation, a respectable married man in jeopardy. He had the sense to recoil and recognise the difficulty of it in order to be able to act out the part.

Rose became more and more jealous of Claudia as time went by, and she didn't like Andrew talking on the phone to her. She had only met Claudia once but that was enough to know that she was very attractive and sophisticated. She was single and not bound by any ties. She worked in the local estate agents office and shared a flat with her best friend. They had moved up from the London area in search of the quieter, less congested countryside round Cumbria.

She was not a born and bred Cumbrian and neither was she a through and through true English rose. She had a strain of Indian blood in her veins descended from her great grandfather who had been a sergeant in the British Army in India when the country was part of the British Empire. He had met and married a local girl when posted there in the mid 1800's. Andrew had no way of knowing about it but he did wonder.

Rose had been so carefree and happy in their first years together, that for this to come between them was like a cloud that wouldn't go away. She tried to concentrate on her work in the community, on her flower arranging engagements and on the W.I. meetings as a member of the committee. It was not enough to stop her feeling the niggling suspicion she had about Claudia. It was envy which, in any shape or form is destructive. She recognised that it was harmful but could not help herself. Envy happens everywhere and can even rear its ugly head in nursery school.

Andrew liked them both and he wanted to please them both. Maybe the honourable thing to do would be to give in, admit the reason and hand over the part to his understudy. He couldn't do that because he was a showman. He wanted the glory of being the leading man and it was such a good part for him. He was cast as a debonair man about town and it suited his character to play a suave young gentleman.

It was also a step up the ladder in the world of Amateur acting. One day, perhaps in the not too far distant future he was ambitious enough to want to produce a play, and then to even write one. There was one night he nearly blew it all, met his nemesis so to speak and just managed to save himself.

All the other actors had left and he and Claudia were alone in the back room behind the stage. He turned round and there she was, in front of him. He came very close to kissing her in the privacy and seclusion of the moment, just managing to resist the temptation. He shuffled away to the open door and with.

"See you next week," he disappeared into the dark night. He managed to start the car and to drive home with the certain knowledge that if it had happened it would have undermined his confidence He knew that he would then have been unable to carry on. His conscience was clear but he knew very well that he had been very close to succumbing to the desire that bugged him.

Rose continued to be jealous of Claudia. It seemed that her husband wasn't interested in her anymore. She lost the impetus to make the most of herself and the dresses that he had admired did not please her. The many compliments he had paid her seemed empty and the former magic of their relationship had disappeared.

There was one day when she could only compare her mood with the sorry story of the slug that had climbed out of the plant pot she had placed on the hearth. It had been in search of damp as the plant where it had lived had shrivelled and died. The poor thing found itself on the alien dryness of the rug with a thick pile. It had left a thin silver thread on its journey across the length of it and back again The end came when it went round and round in a desperate circle, finally finishing in the death throws, a sticky little pool of wetness on the mat. The animal was exhausted and beaten.

It was something she could not share with Andrew because of what the scenario had meant to her in her lone state. Where they had originally delighted in sharing their innermost doubts and ideas, they suddenly had secrets from each other; that was the pity of it.

Chapter 20

All the fields on the farm were enclosed by dry stone walls that had to be maintained. Now and then there occurred the job of repairing a piece where it had collapsed and left a gap in the wall. It was on one of those rebuilding jobs when Andrew was out alone in the field with the opportunity to do quite a lot of day dreaming.

It was a lovely summers' day with hardly a cloud in the sky, and he was sitting on the grass with his picnic that had been put up for him by Rose. Some of the stones off the wall were lying in a heap beside him, still to sort and assess for the rest of the job in hand. It was a case of carefully selecting them to fit tightly together, by no means an easy task. The irregular shaped stones were all sizes and they had to be turned over in the hand as they were fitted into the wall. It had to be secure and even, and there had to be enough of the correct size and shape left to finish off the top of the wall. It had to correspond and to look as though there had never been a repair job. There was still quite a lot to do and he had to finish before the end of the day. The following day he would take himself off on some jaunt.

Sitting there in the otherwise empty field he was in a reverie. He gazed ahead into the distance but his thoughts were elsewhere. In another month he would be thirty and that was something to ponder on. It was a sobering thought to be leaving his youth behind. He reflected on it on what he had achieved and what he hoped to achieve.

He found himself thinking about Claudia in her office and wondering if she might be thinking about him. He tried to imagine how she might look as she sat at her desk. She was roughly the same age while Rose was a bit younger. He thought a lot about their performance on the stage as always. He congratulated himself on making it such a convincing and dramatic story, wondering how it could be perfected in some way. It kept coming back to him to occupy his days and nights as it did that day alone in the field.

He eventually got round to thinking about Rose and tried to picture her in his mind's eye, either working in the kitchen or in the garden. He thought about her wanting a baby and about himself with a baby son or daughter. He wanted that too. It hadn't happened yet. He could comprehend how it would be fulfilling for her, and he hoped to make her happy some day by keeping focused on creating a family. With that thought in his head he turned to thinking about going back and then to loving her.

He sat a while longer in a vacant mood but he must get on for there was still a lot to do at the wall. As he sat he had watched a solitary crow and had thrown it a crust from his lunch box. They were not carrion crows but he still didn't like them. They nested in the tops of the trees in the next village and there were too many of them. It strutted about before him, jerking its head back and forth as it walked its halting walk, waiting for another crust. It had finally given up and flown off.

The completion of the wall was difficult for he desperately wanted to pack up. Yet he had to concentrate and finish the job properly before he allowed himself to leave it and return home to his Rose.

At last he was able to stand back from it and to observe that to anyone else it would not have been apparent there had been a repair job. He was pleased with his work and he knew how to identify the place by a mound in the ground almost half way along the length of the wall. He would show Rose his days work another time.

Chapter 21

One tremendous bonus to living in the Appleby district for Rose was to be close to her beloved grandmother. At the testing time she was experiencing it was to be the healing balm that helped her overcome the difficulty. Her mother and father in Kendal had been so happy and so proud of her match with whom they regarded the best son-in-law imaginable. She didn't want to disillusion them so she had kept the quarrel a secret and pretended that everything was as it should be. It wasn't a quarrel either but an unfortunate turn of events that had come between Andrew and her. If she had sought some professional advice (which she didn't for one minute think of doing) they would have told her that it was a passing fancy and that it would all come right. She was fairly sure that would have been how they would view it. She had to struggle with the loneliness and problem herself with no one to confide in.

She wasn't going to tell her grandmother either but Ellen was observant and wise enough to surmise that something had come between the pair. She was wise enough also, not to ask questions or to probe her granddaughter's marriage problems. She knew from her own experience of life that things were best left to work themselves out sometimes and, 'the less said, the better' was a good code to abide by.

Ellen was just as welcoming and kind as she could be to her beloved and very precious Rose. Her grandmother's home and the village where she lived were very dear to Rose as she had gone there all her young life. It had been at the beginning with her mother when she was a child and then by herself, and to be able to go there at that crucial time was most wonderful and most helpful to her.

She knew the place so well that she felt a part of it, and she was especially familiar with the plants in the garden. There were some quite rare ones too. She knew that neither Mahonia nor Arcanthus were the easiest plants to grow but once established they both thrive well without much attention. There they were in the garden, the Mahonia in the front and the Arcanthus in the border at the back of the house. Both have spectacular foliage that is a feature and both have a kind of statuesque quality.

Other plants in the garden were Bleeding Heart, a vivid blue iris of gigantean proportion, Lily of the Valley, Spirea, a red Peony, Rose of Sharon, Japanese Anemone, Columbine, Phlox, the everlasting silver flower, Esther Reed, Fuchsia, Hostas and the more common rhododendron and Azalea shrubs and a variety of roses. In the early spring there grew a continuous row of daffodils that had been planted along by the roadside in the front of the bungalow. There were snowdrops everywhere, not only in Ellen's garden but down by the beck that ran through the village

Flowers were very much part of Ellen's life as well as her granddaughters. There were always some cut flowers or some plant in the lounge. Rose had used many of them in her flower arrangements at some time or another. In the autumn there was quite a lot to do in Ellen's garden where all the herbaceous plants had to be cut back along the borders to the side and to the back of the house. That was where Rose was able to help. For anyone who was unfamiliar with the plants, it would just have been tedious but for her who knew how the flowers had looked when they were blooming, it was something else.

She had seen the garden in all seasons and she knew that, although the frosts and snow might come and cover the plants, they would come alive again in early spring and small shoots would begin to appear. That was the magic of a garden. The wonderful beauty of the herbaceous border was that it never failed and even severe frosts did not kill the resilient plants. There was an ongoing wealth of interest throughout the spring and summer months. It only began to wane and fade at the beginning of September.

On a visit to the bungalow one day Rose was sitting on the garden seat at the front of the house after doing some work in the garden. When all else was quiet there intervened and became played out a curious little interlude about her feet. She kept very still and didn't even move her head for out of the corner of her eye she glimpsed the slow, penetrating and amazing approach of a solitary little hedgehog. It had evidently travelled along the flags in front of the bungalow, and came round to the stone trough where the annuals are always planted, and to the back of the wooden seat where Rose was seated.

She kept very still and although there was no sound, she sensed that the little creature was sniffing at the heels of her leather shoes. Then it reappeared the way it had come and she watched its slow progress to the edge of the rockery before her. She could see how it walked with its characteristic pointed nose, and the two little back feet that were protruding from the prickly oval shaped body. Never having seen a hedgehog at close quarters before, let alone one on the move, was something of a surprise. It had been an especially magic moment that was a surprise.

It had been a magical appearance that was totally unexpected. Hedgehogs are a very shy animal, easily frightened and not often seen in broad daylight. There was suddenly the knowledge of there being one in her grandmother's garden and might even be more. Rose would go and tell her about it.

She looked forward to getting the loathsome play over and done with, and then there would be a chance of getting her Andrew back to herself again. She didn't blame him entirely as plenty of women in her situation would have done. To be fair it was all an unfortunate catastrophe but she had so far managed to keep her cool, and that was most commendable. It had not been easy when she had to fight on herself with her conviction and suspicion with no one to confide in. When it was all over, then she might spill the beans, and talk to Alice at Kendal about the trauma she had endured.

There was one more hurdle on the horizon which was the actual week of the performance. She didn't want to see the play but she knew she was expected to go to see her husband in his role of lead actor. People would think it strange if she didn't. It was a matter of keeping up appearances.

Andrew was not insensitive to his wife's jealousy of Claudia, and his own conscience told him that it was understandable too. He knew she was unhappy about going to see it. The first three nights of the production had gone by with little communication between them. There were only two more left before it all finished.

When he arrived back home from the third performance he asked her, "You'll come tomorrow night to see me, Rose?" Then he pleaded, "You've got to come tomorrow. It means so much to me for you to be there."

He spoke very quietly, in almost a whisper. For one thing he was tired with the effort of acting the three nights, and because he was literally begging her into submission.

She replied "I will come on your last night, I promise."

He was satisfied and got quietly into bed.

When she joined him he got very close to her warm body, she understood his need and allowed herself to be a kind of comforting solace in his exhaustion. They slept in some sort of understanding and harmony that night. It was in her generous nature to act that way, and to put her faith in him and in the belief that everything would come right.

She had dreamed about Claudia a lot. She knew about the angry scene they acted out together. She even knew the actual word for word script for she had helped Andrew with learning his part at the beginning. Sometimes it seemed as if their roles were reversed, that Claudia was the real wife and she the fictitious one. That was why she had taken to going over to her grandmother where she was able to get out of her own environment, and get interested in doing something useful that took her away. She could then stop thinking about the obsession and be less introspective.

Chapter 22

Rose did as she was bid and got ready for the final night's performance of the play that had been such a protracted trial for her. She was glad that it would soon be over. As always when she went out she took time to get ready, and as Andrew had left early she had no one to hinder her. Her mid brown hair had a natural tendency to curl which meant that all it ever needed was a brush and comb to style it. Hair like hers was a great asset as her mother had often told her.

She never wore much jewellery and sometimes didn't wear any but that night she put on the pearl and diamante earrings given to her by Andrew for her birthday. She complemented them with her double string of pearls at the neckline of her favourite dress in blue and mauve to shades of purple, made of a fine woollen cloth. She could have had a seat on the front row but chose to sit on an end seat half way down the hall.

Andrew was well aware of his wife's presence and he was therefore more articulate in his performance as well as more guarded. When it came to the kitchen scene where he and Claudia were at each other's throats, he was supposed to get hold of her arm and hold it rigid in a vice like grip, which he had done convincingly on previous nights. He merely lightly touched the sleeve of her dress. She was begging him to take her back.

He was saying, "I am warning you. If you should ever see that man again you will be thrown out of this house, and you will never come back."

At that point Claudia waited with her hand half raised, and she was dismayed and bemused when Andrew didn't grab her in the usual way. In fact she was nearly thrown off balance but managed to gain her equilibrium, remember her words and continue. The episode was noticed by the producer who had to work out as to why the scene had been toned down by his leading man. The play carried on with Claudia beseeching to be given another chance.

"Take me back. I won't let you down again."

The producer watched with rapt attention afterwards. At the end of the performance there was a surprise for everyone. Other nights the curtain had gone up on all the actors standing in a row with Andrew and Claudia in the centre, and all holding hands.

This final night turned out to be different. Andrew took the initiative to stand forward of his own accord without an invitation and to address the audience.

He began, "My wife is here tonight amongst you."

With that, he stepped down off the stage to where Rose was seated. He took her by the hand and led her up onto the stage and to the forefront of all the other actors.

"My Rose."

She had been dragged along by her determined husband and now took centre stage before a rapt audience. They were watching something being played out which was unrehearsed and was therefore interesting; something that was personal.

Andrew collected his wits together and continued, "My lovely Rose who has helped me all the way; who has been so supportive. I owe everything to Rose."

By that time everyone was cheering and clapping. Someone in the audience shouted, "Three cheers for Rose," and there followed three cheers. The curtain came down on the cast, then up again and down for the final time. Rose had been right next to Claudia but it was all fine and there were no hard feelings that night.

The hall had been almost full. The final night was a resounding success, and that little inspired finale by Andrew honouring his adored wife (known already by quite a lot of people) had put a personal stamp on the performance. Andrew was the man of the moment who stood out as a leader, and someone to be looked up to as a leader, and someone to be looked up to in the community. His reputation and integrity were intact, and the success of the play was everything that mattered. They went home together to celebrate. He had made it so far and he would carry on with his plan to further his notoriety as a public figure through the media of Amateur Dramatics.

Chapter 23

Rose was looking back on the night of the play much as a bride would remember her wedding day, with the sweet taste of achievement and glory as if it had been her moment as well as her husband's.

It had been such a lonely time when she had felt isolated and left out, that to be brought forward into the limelight and acknowledged was a triumph. She was glad it happened the way it did, glad that the play was over and done with.

She was also proud to be Mrs Forbes and proud of Andrew's success and his popularity. She didn't think about Claudia being around for the next production either. In fact she had been steadily courting a policeman as it turned out. The chances were that she would never again be cast to play such an intimate and challenging scene with Andrew. Rose needn't have worried for before the end of the year was through she would have left the district anyway.

Rose would never know the absolute truth of how near her husband had been to making a total hash of his ambition and plans that night when they were alone in the anteroom after the rehearsal. He knew too well, and knew how he wouldn't have had the gall to live a lie and carry on acting. He was very pleased with himself, with his reception that last night of the play, and he was grateful and proud of his charming little wife. The whole episode had brought them closer together and in harmony with each other.

People were congratulating him on his performance and saying how they had enjoyed the play. It was generally very heart warming and encouraging. He even began to think about inventing a story, and eventually writing a play. He remembered what one of the teachers had said at the Grammar School, "You can do anything if you try."

Although Rose did not think about Claudia being around for the next production by the Amateur Dramatic Society, she was still not ready to forget the trauma of it all. As she had gone over to help her grandmother during the lonely days when she seemed left out of Andrew's life, she carried on going after the play was over. She was in a much happier frame of mind, and it didn't go unnoticed by Ellen who was quick to see how her granddaughter's mood had changed. She had asked no questions but had suspected something was wrong with her home life.

Now she wanted to be told the reason for the singing Rose for that was what she was doing. Ellen could overhear her as she dug the garden in the back border. Rose was singing a joyful song for a reason, she was celebrating.

Lately she had become aware of a change in herself. She was fairly sure she was going to have the baby she wanted. The first person to know should have been Andrew but she had deliberately not told him for she had not had enough time to forget about his lack of feeling for her when he had been taken up with the play and Claudia.

It could have happened soon after the night when it had seemed such a triumph both for him and for her. Still being bruised by the experience and the neglect she would just be a bit reserved, and enjoy keeping a secret for a while. She was rather afraid of carrying a baby but it was alright in the early days of a pregnancy.

She supposed she would cope with it when it happened. Then she was caught out putting some dates down on the back of a letter. Her grandmother asked her outright, "You couldn't be working something out, Rose, could you?"

Rose looked up and met her gaze, "It is a secret," she answered.

"You should tell your mother, Rose. She will be delighted for you."

That night she went home and told her husband and he guessed she had known for some time. It had been a joyous time working away in the garden with the secret knowledge all to herself. Andrew knew then that she had a grudge against him but he didn't say.

They discussed names and were both happy and united.

Chapter 24

It was that time of year just before the onset of winter when the last leaves of autumn were about to blow off the trees that Rose had enjoyed some walks around the village of Ormsby. Her favourite one was to continue further up the road from Ellen's bungalow. It went past the farm where she and her husband had lately farmed. There was a stone milk stand by the roadside that had stood the test of time, no longer then in use and gathering moss but likely to last for centuries to come.

There were some more dwellings that constituted that part of the village called Townhead and the narrow lane continued on through parallel hedges. The first frosts had arrived one morning on her walk, and there were faint cobwebs hung with jewel-like vapour glistening in the autumnal sunlight.

The lane held much of interest for her for she liked to study the plants and the colours. Even the tree trunks had subtle colouring in shades of pale blue, greys, and light browns.

The dykes had mostly been laid back and some of the horizontal growths were like great arms, entwined and moss covered. In certain places the dykes finished up in a tangle of twigs, and were covered by a web of the sticky sweetheart vegetation that clung to everything. It was all interesting to her.

She had occasionally seen a squirrel running across the road or climbing up a tree. One incongruous sight was an old iron bed head that had been put there to fill a gap in the hedge. It was a symbol of how important and urgent the necessity to keep the animals from straying.

One day Rose happened to be at the far end of the road when the red Post Office delivery van arrived. The tarmac came to an end where there were two gates leading to two farms that were reached across rough tracks.

The postman had to stop his van, open the gate, drive through, and get out again shutting the gate. That was one of the hazards in such country places where the gates have to be kept shut.

Another time Rose had witnessed feeding a field full of sheep on the lane. The bogey had passed her in the lane. Before it even got through the field gate, the whole flock of sheep heard and recognised the familiar sound of the engine. With one accord they all start running towards the feeding trough. There were the black Jacob sheep as well as the more usual white ones. Quite a few of them were lame but the lame ones managed to keep up with the others in their hurry to be there at feeding time. It had been a real spectacle to watch.

The spring of that year was a good time. Andrew devoted all his energies to looking after Rose during the months of waiting, and not going off on day trips so much. He directed his attention to the prospect of a baby in the house, and to taking on the responsibilities of being a parent. That was for the time being. Rose coped very well with the pregnancy which gave her little trouble, and a little blue-eyed baby boy arrived two weeks early in the month of June. They had decided on Jonathan for a name. Andrew's need to project his own image was there still. Rose knew that much about the man she married, and that was what turned out to be the exciting thing about her life. She never knew quite what was going to happen.

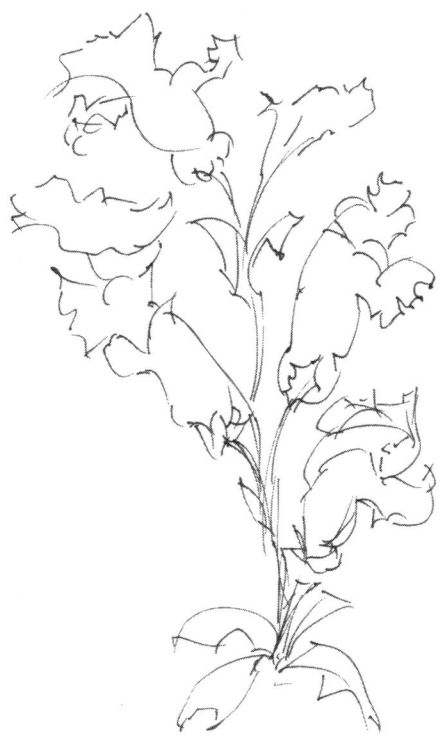